THE UNRAVELING MYSTERY OF THE ILLUSIVE FOREST

A JOURNEY TO UNCOVER THE SECRETS

SREERUP CHAKRABORTY

Made with ♥ on the Notion Press Platform
www.notionpress.com

ॐ श्री गणेशाय नमः

To my beloved family and friends, who have always supported me in my innovative journey. I want to give a special dedication to my grandfathers, **Sir. Ajit Chakraborty** *and* **Sir. Dhanapati Banerjee**, *who have both passed away. Although I never had the chance to know Sir Ajit Chakraborty more, his lessons continue to inspire me. To my other grandfather, thank you for always being there for me and instilling in me a love of fantasy. This book is also dedicated to my parents, who embody strength, resilience, and unconditional love. Your unwavering support has been my greatest source of inspiration. A special thanks to my wife Suvadra, who has been my constant supporter on my innovative journey. This book is dedicated to all of you, with all my heart and gratitude.*

Additionaly, In memory of the late writer Shri Asish Basu, who told me about Notion Press.

Contents

Introduction

Welcome to the mystical world of fiction, where imagination and creativity have no bounds. Our story takes place in a lush and dense forest that is home to a tribe that has lived there for generations, as well as a forest officer named Aniruddha. However, there is more to this forest than its natural treasures. Deep within it, a God-gifted object capable of producing supernatural powers is hidden. Many covet this object, including the forces of evil.

As the story unfolds, we follow the quest of a Himalayan monk, Shyam, Aniruddha, and a driver who come together to find the object and protect it from the devil's gaze. The headman of the tribe, other members of the community, and the Seven Immortals also have a role in safeguarding the forest and its resources.

This story is a journey filled with adventure, intrigue, and the battle between good and evil. As the group works to keep the power of the object hidden, they must navigate the forest without attracting the attention of the Seven Immortals, who have been guarding the forest for centuries.

While this story is a work of fiction, it draws inspiration from both science and spirituality. The central belief of the Seven Immortals, a Hindu religious belief, plays a significant role in the story. It is not about tips, tricks, or success spells. It is a journey of discovering the secrets of a superpower and the problems that come with it. Through this work of fiction, I hope to convey a message that inspires and encourages readers to face their own challenges with courage and resilience.

Disclaimer

I am bowing to my inner god as I present to you my first novel, "The Unravelling Mystery of The illusive Forest". This story has been with me for the past five years, and it is finally time to share it with the world. As a beginner author, I have tried my best to weave together an intricate tale that combines science, spirituality, and fantasy. In this story, I delve into the concept of a superpower and explore the complexities that come with possessing such abilities. Through the story's many twists and turns, I hope to impart valuable lessons for readers to take away and apply to their own lives. I want to make it clear that this story does not aim to harm or criticize any religion, belief, or scientific invention. It is simply a work of fiction that draws inspiration from a variety of sources. it carries many lessons to learn and enjoy the world of fantasy. While there are some references to Hindu gods, They are treated with utmost respect and reverence. I want to clarify that this story is not about tips, tricks, or success spells. It is about the journey of discovering the secrets of a superpower and the problems that come with it. I have taken inspiration from science and spirituality, and have tried to convey a message through this work of fiction. I want to make it clear that a natural intoxication is mentioned in this book for illustrative purposes, I do not condone or encourage any form of addiction. As a work of fantasy, I have endeavored to bring the story to life, but I want to be clear that addiction is harmful and not to be taken lightly. As a new author, I acknowledge that my writing may have some mistakes. However, I hope that readers can look past these errors and instead focus on the underlying message of the story. The story is easy to understand.Then no race was looked down upon here. I have included a Sanskrit verse that is not referenced from any particular source, but rather an original creation of my imagination.I would like to extend my gratitude to all my readers for taking the time to read my book. I welcome any feedback, whether it be through email, social media, or other means.your important feedback will help me to improve mistakes. I hope that this story touches your heart and soul, just as it has mine.

Thank you for joining me on this journey.

Sincerely,

Sreerup Chakraborty

Acknowledgements

First and foremost, I must thank those who introduced me to the English language, such as my mother, my primary and secondary school teachers. I am deeply grateful to **Prof. DK Chattopadhyay**, who has shown me through their own struggles that it is possible to keep fighting and overcome obstacles. Their example has been a constant source of strength and motivation for me.

And Thanks to Karna Mukherjee. I used his picture on the cover.

Thought

Writing this book has been a challenging but fulfilling journey for me. Throughout the process, I faced numerous obstacles that tested my determination and focus. There were times when I struggled to find the right words, or when I was simply too busy with daily life to make progress. In addition, I initially wrote this story in Bengali, and it had some variations compared to this English version. The original story had more characters and a larger scope, but for this book, I have condensed the plot while preserving the essence of the story. Despite the challenges, I am grateful for the opportunity to share this story with readers. And I hope that this book will be the first step in a long and fulfilling journey as an author.I want to acknowledge that this is my first attempt at writing a story in English, and there may be mistakes in grammar and vocabulary. I have tried my best to convey the story and its message accurately, But if any senior author or reader finds any errors or has suggestions for improvement, I welcome your feedback and guidance. This book is the product of my passion and effort, and I hope that it brings joy and entertainment to all those who read it.In this story, It was a warm summer evening when I first came up with the idea for this book. I was sitting in my garden, lost in thought, when I realized that I wanted to share my fiction story with the world. This book is the result of that realization. Throughout my life, I have faced many challenges and obstacles. But through perseverance and determination, I have overcome them and emerged stronger. I have learned that "it is not the challenges we face that define us, but how we choose to respond to them". In this book, I think the characters we create in our minds are really children of our mind. I invite you to join me on this journey, and to discover the lessons and insights that lie within these pages. I hope this book will not only entertain but also offer valuable lessons for its readers. I believe that every person has a story to tell, and I am honored to share mine with you. I also run a small YouTube channel called 'Jene Rakho' where we create informative videos for our audience. I am grateful for the love and support I have received from my viewers and would like to encourage new viewers to check out our channel.

I want to thank my readers, who have taken the time to read this book. I hope that it touches your heart and soul, as it has mine.

Thank you for reading.

Sincerely,

Sreerup Chakraborty

CHAPTER ONE

The Unravelling Mystery of The illusive Forest

Many years ago a monk came from the Himalayas. He was a predictor and possessed all powers. He achieved all divine and demonic power. There is no pursuit (Sadhana) in the world that he has not done. He did all the pursuit starting from hard meditation for the goddess Kali. Whatever we call him, Tantric, Aghori, it is somewhat less. Everyone knows that pursuit is not cheap. But he was very proficient in all kinds of realization.But even after knowing all this, he never used any part of his Power for any evil purpose. He was looking for the purpose, how to use the power of good. He was looking for a wise and truly selfless man. But it was very difficult to find such a person. In today's age, if someone gets such divine power, he will do something so destructive without thinking that the world is about to be destroyed. In other words, he will become a demon. He wants to be the king of the whole world also after a few days he will think of heaven. As per various Puranas, various Asuras after becoming extremely powerful only tried to control the entire universe. Then, of course, he had to die for some reason or the other, be it at the hands of goddess Durga, or Brahma-Vishnu-Mahesh. If there is such an evil mentality, He must fall. Who would want someone to break the things he has worked hard to build? It's pretty much like that. So that monk was looking for someone who would use it for some educational work and use this power to save the whole world from its enemies from some secret place. He traveled almost all over world on foot and eventually reached the right place.An unidentified Forest, Where a person was looking for a saint who could answer all his questions. Aniruddha Sabyasachi, Age 30 a forest officer and researcher. In his ancestral home, there is no one. His childhood life was very difficult; he could not identify his father. His mother died during his birth, and he grew up with his "Daima" (A woman skilled in aiding the delivery of babies.), then studied on scholarship and got this job. He sends most of his salary to Daima, Daima's two daughters, Kamala and Saraswati, Kamala got married last year.Aniruddha was looking for something that, once he got it, he could do things that were very difficult to do. No one wanted to stay easily in the place where his duty was. So he was in a high position in that office. Because there was no heavy population up to 50 km of this forest, except for one tribal group. It is forbidden to mention the name of this forest. Because it is a secret forest. It is not available on the map. Repository of all organic medicines mentioned by Veda. Moreover, some plants are highly addictive when ingested. Which is only used by the residents here from generation to generation it is only their right because they make medicine with it and protect it for a long time. These tribal groups are not like ordinary tribal group, they are very dangerous, according to them The seven Immortals is their god, and they celebrate the "Sanata" festival every year. Tribal allows only one outsider to stay in this forest and he is Anirudha. Besides, many other officers came here, but none could handle the greed for money, so they had to leave here with punishment. The only one they looked good on and gave him all kinds of help and love. Now, the two Aniruddha and the monk are finding each other, Some times letter the monk has come near the forest. Aniruddha is staying inside the forest. No one knows what is going to happen now, the tribal is surrounded by the forest, and the monk understands this very well. But anyhow he had to enter. On the other side, meanwhile near a reservoir, Anirudha is telling stories to the locals. They love to hear such stories; women are busy with household chores, But they are listening to the story of Aniruddha. He explains the difference between science and spirituality. "Ordinary people will not be able to do anything for the sake of this science. What is, in this nature can only be done from those. But they have no power to bring any power from outside. Nor, science is capable of creating a second sun, moon, or other planets. An airplane created by science is an object that travels in the sky. A rocket goes from one planet to another. But does he have the power to go for the past or future? Simply no. Because the laws of nature do not allow for building a time machine. Science has successfully invented robot, where the brain is programmed in such a way that it behaves like a human being, but it also has an end, and if it falls into the hands of a bad person, it will do something very destructive. Therefore, without a human being, that robot will not be able to do any good in the world."

The headman and many others listened with full concentration

Aniruddha continued. - “If all the people in the world were to die and only robots remained, the world as we know it would cease to exist. Even with advanced programming, robots can never truly replicate human behavior. Humans are unique in that we are made up of five elements - fire, water, air, sky, and earth. While science has made incredible advances, it cannot create a physical person with the same complexities as a living human being”

Silence descended upon the group, as it seemed that no one was willing to speak up in favor of science. In the meantime, the Headman took a cannabis clay pipe from an elderly man, smoked it after chanting a secret mantra, and then asked, "And then what?"

Aniruddha continued, "No matter how much science has accomplished, it cannot create a human being or give them life after death. And it cannot replicate the unique composition of the human body, made up of five elements."

However, before the story could come to an end, a commotion broke out, and everyone’s attention was lost. Aniruddha stood up, and the group became tense. The commotion was caused by guards catching an outsider in the forest. The guards dragged the monk directly to the forest court, and he didn’t look once at the headman but kept his eyes on Aniruddha. The atmosphere was tense, and the headman was crowned with the responsibility of settling the conflict. Aniruddha served as a special adviser, and the headman crowned him as well. Previously, some foreigners had tried to steal medicinal plants from the forest, and they were detained for ten years before being handed over to the administration.

The headman questioned the monk, "Why did you come here? Don’t you know it’s forbidden?"

The monk replied, "Yes, sir, I know. But there was no other way. I didn't come to steal or to stay. I came from the Himalayas. I can freeze your throne instantly. Would you like to see?"

The headman ordered his immediate arrest, declaring him an enemy. However, Aniruddha raised his hand and interjected, "No, he's innocent. I don't believe he's our enemy. Let him prove his innocence."

Aniruddha raised his hand and addressed the headman and the monk, "Wait, this man may have something important to share with us. Let him speak and tell us why he had to come to this forbidden land. And let us hear him out before we judge him.

Now the monk moved his left hand forward without saying a word and said a spell and immediately headman got up from his throne. Everyone present there was amazed. Headman's throne has turned into ice. Everyone standing in the forest court stood in a bowing posture. the headman was very happy. He realized that if the monk had intended to be hostile, then he wouldn't be caught by our guard. The tribal drum started playing all around. Judgment completed. Headman conceded defeat to the monk and he wanted to hand over his judicial crown to the monk. But the monk respected the headman and said

-why are you doing this? I am your unknown guest you have the right to verify me. I would like to speak to your special advisor.

Headman said -ok you talk. We are preparing some food for both of you. Then the headman and others left, and now the monk and Aniruddha started talking.

Aniruddha asked the monk, -tell me now who are you and what have you come for?

The Monk said, -What name should I tell you, I have 108 names. You do one thing instead you make my name 109. You give me a name.

Aniruddha said, ok I will give, but first you tell me how you know me?

The monk said, listion, nothing is unknown to me. I've worked so hard, and full of my life that it's not too difficult for me to know a person and every person I see on the street has an identity that pops up in front of me and I'm looking for someone, maybe you're the one, I can give something. In my eyes, you are the one person to whom I can give powers to you. after getting that power you will save this world from the enemy.

Aniruddha asked -What kind of power? I am researching spiritual science.

The monk said, yes, you don't have to say anything I know everything you are researching how to connect with Gods how to get the power of those Gods, and do well for nature.

Aniruddha said That's right. But I have some questions that maybe you can answer.

The monk said, Of course, I will answer all your questions but I have come a long way now and My life is going to go out in any direction due to hunger and thirst. Now don't bother me with these questions. I will answer all your questions. Please arrange some food and some water. A little sleep is also not bad.

Aniruddha said, Yes, yes of course they have arranged food for you, you come with me. The monk said, Ohh! What a pleasant environment you live in, I can't explain, you live in this house? Aniruddha said yes, they made it, especially for me.

The tribal made a house for Aniruddha, but it is not a concrete house, they built a round shape wall with a sequence of a lot of thick tree trunks and bamboo. All this design planning was done by the headman; he is no less than a civil engineer. The rooftop is also made in a strange peaked shape. Water-resistant, storm proof and temperature controlled, The floor is made up of small pieces of stone that have been rubbed together to make it look like a marble floor. Two windows, a large door, a bamboo bed, a sofa, a table chair, a bookcase, and some weapon storage. In one place there is a rope, a net, a rifle, and some bullets. However, that's not been used for a long time. Meanwhile, there is a radio phone on the table. There is also a special secret forest map. The big yard of the house is decorated with various flowers and fruit trees, there is a sweet smell of cannabis flowers all around. The yard of the house is also paved with stones like the floor. A narrow road leads straight to a ruined concrete house. That was the forest office; this road is made So that the mud does not accumulate during rain. However, everything in the Forest Office has now been shifted to this house. Because the office is ruined, waterfalls. They didn't fix it, because they didn't like this kind of house at all. Here river water is consumed as drinking water, and Bee nectar and rolled cotton are used to light the house at night. The food here is white Sitashal rice, poppy seeds, various vegetables, and river fish fry.

The Monk and Aniruddha Ate, It is now afternoon but there is no way to know the time Because last month Aniruddha`s watch has gone damaged. The monk is resting. Little boys and girls are hanging from the Banyan tree prop root. Aniruddha is reading a book. The women are watching the little boys play, some women breastfeed their babies, Young men are guarding the forest, some men cut dry wood, and the headman smokes cannabis. The rules here are very strict. If we talk about intoxication. Drinking alcohol is not allowed here. They only consume cannabis but Forest guards are prohibited from consuming cannabis while on duty, youths are not allowed to smoke, except after shifting duty they only get cannabis drink.

Now the monk stands up from sleep. Aniruddha closed the book and asked the monk,

-do you need anything?

Monk said -come here I have something to show you. Aniruddha was outside and when he entered the room he was shocked by what he saw

A variety of sweets, many laddus, were arranged in bowls on the floor of the room.

Aniruddha asked -where this comes from. Who came here?

The monk said, -Give them to all and you eat, I created them with my magic. You are doing so much for good and your research is also worthwhile so today I thought if I can feed you some good food then my efforts will also be worthwhile because it is very difficult to find good people like you.

Aniruddha said, why you went to do this, you can use your power for any good. By doing so much to feed me, you will suffer, I don't need so much. Two times boiled rice, little fried vegetables, a little fruit is enough for me, please don't do this in future.

The monk said I came to you, I will not give you anything? I will leave like this? I may not be able to give you so much gold, gems, or money because even if I could, they would be against my pursuit, but I can at least feed you a little while I am here.

Aniruddha said, where do you go? If I let you go.

The monk said My son, don't hold me I have to go I'm a monk It's not my nature to stay in one place Today here tomorrow there Today I'm in the mountains Tomorrow in the sea. This is how I live. Yes, my son, I can't sit in a specific place, You test first, then we will talk more.

Aniruddha called two people from outside and distributed the sweets to everyone, everyone was very happy to get such delicious sweets.

Another one came to see if there was more, and Aniruddha told him there was no more.

Aniruddha asked At one time I tried a lot of meditation but when I saw that I could not do it, I started doing this research to see if there is anything at all or if I just wasting my time. But when you came, faith was born in me slowly but I don't know how long that faith will last. The monk said You are quite right on your part. Because even if you try, you will never get the vision or possess any power that you have been looking for or that you want to get through sadhana. But yes you can get something that you do not want. Aniruddha asked But what will I get, that living this way will not have any result? Leaving the house, I am so far away in a lonely forest. The fight I am fighting will not be successful? The monk said you understand the meaning of sacrifice, why not? All will be worthwhile, why did I come? I was looking for you. Now that I've found you, I'm going to give you some information that you don't know. I will tell you what you failed to write about your research and point out some of your mistakes. I will fill your book. See my son, to know God first you have to know the secret of this whole nature, to know that secret you have to experience this nature. I will take you to a place where you will realize how wrong you were. When you go there, you can never imagine what you will see. Aniruddha said, are there any places that I am not visited? You new here, you show me something I haven't seen before?

You have not visited the place. which is a hidden place.

As soon as he spoke he said to the monk, wait a bit, I will come after and tell the headman that we are going into the deep forest. well, Can't we go tomorrow morning?

The monk said, no my son, only you can visit at night

Aniruddha went to the headman and started telling this matter, it was seen that the headman was not taking it well, looking at the monk with raised eyebrows.

after hearing everything he said, "No, I will not let you go at night, or if you have to go, I will go with you.", The monk said it is not possible, hey headman, I have taken his responsibility, it is his sole pursuit. But it will also need your help, you keep people ready, and if we sense danger we will signal you with counsel, I don't want to use any supernatural powers of this nature due to the law of this nature. the headman was somewhat reassured by the monk's words and said, "Well then, go ahead." We will be ready. the monk and Aniruddha entered the deep forest. Walking along Aniruddha asks, well, there are so many astrologers all over the world, so many planet-star experts, astrologers are roaming around, well, are these true or are they just rumors, just an attempt to open the way to their income?

The monk said they are partly true and partly false. What you see is 3 percent correct out of 100 percent and the remaining 97 percent are completely wrong. Even among those that are accurate, that is not the case with absolute accuracy. If these stones attract any planet, my son, then no one presents a poor person. He might earn a lot of money. If a common man does these things, if he thinks that he can become a millionaire by owning a planet gem, then, this is a wrong idea and he will turn into a beggar my son. There is no need to do them. My son does not believe so much. Because until we understand the real thing, these are nothing it's our foolishness. Aniruddha asked, Another thing I find very confusing, I don't believe them, but I find it very strange that I have seen many people choosing their favorite color, some will read, white. And they believe this is matching with planetary color. So, What is the relationship between planets and stars with these colors? The monk said, colors have no importance in ordinary life but yes when we progress on the spiritual path, colors prove to be of great help to us, such as Black for receive, and white for left.

Walking like this, about 3 hours passed, once the monk became completely silent, suddenly a light started coming out of the monk's body. Such a bright expression has not been seen before

Aniruddha asked, It's been three hours.Where are you going? Where to stay at night? Since then I have been walking, crossing uphill and downhill, hay father Say something, please.

It seems a little strange, it doesn't seem very normal, not like the one he saw three hours ago. As earlier he was answering every question but now he is not answering any question from aniruddha. Aniruddha said again, please tell me something, I am afraid, this forest is so dark, there is no light, there is no weapon, if something comes, how will we face it? I won't go anymore. I can't go more into this forest.

Now the monk said, don't worry, we don't have to go more, You will find all the answers to your questions, look forward.

As Aniruddha looked ahead, his chest began to tremble. his body became cold, such as feeling faint, woozy, weak, or unsteady. Aniruddha asked what is this? I have never seen such an amazing place before. One two three four five six seven, Who is meditating there?

The monk said They are the seven immortal. It is not possible to say how many events they have witnessed. These lamps that you see, my son this oil never runs out, they keep burning for many years, where do you go? It will burn you, don't go ahead, and don't make a mistake that you will regret later. You see that yantra in front, it is a goddess kali yantra. If you get close to it, it will burn you. It is very danger's.aniruddha said, But I want to talk to them. the monk said, Are you crazy? You are delusional. It was a mistake to bring you here. Come on, not for a while. We have to get out of here now. Otherwise, you will meet death. Want to talk to seven immortals as a little ordinary person? This is what happens when you get something without effort

Aniruddha said, Leave me alone I'm ready for it I'll still talk. Please leave me alone.

Now the monk could not control himself and slapped Anirudda's cheek. Even then Aniruddha said again Kill me, kill me, what was the need to show me? Today I will talk. Let me go, I'm not afraid of death, let go, let go

The monk said, Calm down my son calm down. Don't be crazy Do not do what is not possible; otherwise, the danger is inevitable, not only your danger but also the danger can come for the whole world, are you want this?

The monk took him a long way from this place, pulling him by the hand. He put his finger on his forehead and make him unconscious. Then sang the conch to the headman.

The next morning,

Aniruddha woke up after hearing the tribal drum. Aniruddha found himself in his room.

Headman said, we heard the conch and ran but did not see the monk there. Only you were lying there on unconscious condition. Do you know that the python would have eaten you if you were a little late?

A woman brought food on a plate and handed it to

Aniruddha Said to Headman, I am going now from this forest.

-Where are you going?

Himalaya? Said The (suddenly came) monk

Aniruddha did not realize when the monk came between the words of both.

Headman smiled and said, "Go ahead, where you want to go, but you have to come again."

Now the monk said, put one thing in your head very well.

Nothing can be mastered if you are not independent. First, free yourself from any bondage like your job. Not do two things at the same time

Aniruddha asked why? What do you mean?

I need to find an alternative.

Everyone started dancing on four sides.

Tribal drums started.

The monk passed a kush grass mat to Aniruddha's hand and said, Take, sit in meditation.

aniruddha said

this is not possible for me, I tried before, and I said to you yesterday that I have no patience.

The monk said You don't expect anything else from me, I can't give you anything

aniruddha said, What will happen by doing this? I have failed before.

The monk said, You can still try and you won't get the way again.

I thought you were so cool but I didn't know you'd be such stubborn. At this moment you had to bow down yourself to them. If you were to plead with them from afar, it could be that they would call you and then you would go to them. They too have been practicing penance for many,

many years. no,

What did you do? You did the opposite? And I dare to take you somewhere else. ? Go take bath and then sit on Kush grass mat with a pure heart your mind needs to calm down you need to feel first you need to give some promises so next I will take you somewhere or say something else I will leave from here.

Aniruddha took a bath and started a new chapter of his life.

The monk began to teach him various posture, mantras, and various methods. Aniruddha began to learn them at a rapid rate. The monk explained to him that to acquire any supernatural power, it is essential to maintain human stability, otherwise that power will be misused. He also said now I will give you one more realization. Sit on the mudra as I am doing. Aniruddha remained calm and sat in meditation.

This time the monk thrust his ring finger on his head and he winced a little.

He suddenly said, why did you push your finger on my forehead? I got an electric shock.

The monk said, shut up, today I have opened your Ajna chakra, by doing this step by step I will open your 6 chakras. What do you see in front of your eyes now?

In a meditative state, he said a huge tree. Among them are thousands of birdsong. It seems like the birds are trying to tell me something. I don't understand them, I feel them. The monk said, no no no,

don't see the bird, look under the tree, and tell me what you see. He said, I am sitting down, how is it possible? How is it possible? How can I sit? Where is this place, where am I sitting? The monk said Hmm, now you can come out from your meditation.

He came out of meditation and asked, -why did I look like this in meditation?

The monk said, my son, this is what I wanted to show you. This is our basic truth. You probably don't know that billions of people in the world are sitting in the same way under a tree, on a mountain, in a cave, or inside the snow, all of them are meditating. Listen, my son, the purpose of humans, he does not know how many saints there, there are so many sects, so many devotees, so many teachers, but they only say the same thing and these are all stories heard from their predecessors. They don't know the real facts according to them or our liberation is only when the soul merges with the supreme soul. They were also trying to do the same, as soon as they came to the world, they sat down only to try to touch that supreme soul. They have forgotten their purpose in the world.

He asked which place is this, where thousands and millions of such people sit together. Their feet do not hurt, they do not feel hungry, and they do not feel thirsty.

The monk said, Not at all, these are not people who will get sore feet and get thirsty. You may think that you are sitting there but actually, it is not that, your Supreme Soul is sitting there.

He asked, No way to wake him up??

The monk said yes, it can be awakened. Those who have awakened, have become God. They have become masters on earth.

Did he ask, well, is this the real secret of sages or superhumans? They don't just do Meditation, they awaken their Supreme Soul and become the highest rank teacher.

The monk said only to wake him up. if you only wake up then you will be mad. You will know everything and you will not be able to keep your balance. Your energy will increase dramatically. You will not die even if you are very old. You will start to lose control of your energy because you will not understand your purpose and you will not control your energy properly. that's why it's so hard to wake him up.

Aniruuda asked, Well, what exactly can be done after waking him up?

The monk said, what do you want to do? There is nothing in this world that you cannot do. But yes, after doing that, you might regret it. Because there are good and bad in this world. First of all, after getting this power, all the bad forces will try to use you like them. And if you once fall into their hands, you will continue in evil ways, and your destruction is certain. Understand well it is not death it is your destruction.

Aniruddha asked, if I try to wake up or if I wake up then how can I control my energy?

the monk said meditation is the only way to control them. Seek help from your own six senses. For this, you need to awaken.

Even if you don't wake up six chakras, you can wake up. The way to wake him up is also different, but you can't control it. And if you can control, so if you had any state your previous birth, then your six chakras will wake up by themselves.

In this way Aniruddar's meditation continued, once Aniruddar's mind calmed down, he was very different from before. When the monk was meditating, he would stay near the monk so that he would not be disturbed. One day Aniruddha was reading a book, suddenly he saw, some distance away from him there was a round glass, he immediately went up and took the glass and saw that it was a magnifying glass. But a mantra was written inside of it. At that time the monk was cleaning his mated hair. Aniruddha went to him and told him about the mantra, The monk took the glass in his hand and recited the mantra written on it,

पञ्चमणि बल्ल्युक्त धारणे महामहिमा ।
देवप्रिया श्रीयुक्ता असुरलोके प्रोपुजिता।
सः दूरतः पश्यति,
अंगिकार देवस्य समीपम् असमक अखिल-बन्धव। ।

The monk read it and said if this is true then there are many clues here that I had not thought of before. If this is true then we will know many things, which only the God of god, Friends of all, and this unknown person know. It is a verse from an ancient manuscript of the devil; this is usually not available in our world. But I know that the two-piece manuscript came from the devil world, some companions of Koli mistakenly brought, but those two pages could not be found. I heard from my Master, There, some trickery of gods is recorded. It is also written there, how sub-gods will not allow a saint to become a superman in the Koli era, and they will make him a common man.

Aniruddha showed the glass and asked, what does it mean? Tell me a little more.

Thc monk said I can tell you the meaning. But until I know the person who wants to tell you this, it's not the right time to tell you, after hearing you'll be stressed. Be patient, I'll tell you, give me some time.

He filled the special water pot with some water, then he disappeared as he walked. Aniruddha looked at the glass very carefully again but nothing entered his mind, and without thinking anything else he put it down. Now it is noon, and a tribal woman named Parvati gives rice to Aniruddha, Parvati's son Kheta gifted him a golden-colored insect, but Aniruddha releases the insect again. Aniruddha knows that they are children, so they give many such things as gifts. How many times do they bring something, they once caught a tiger cub. He again made them understand that these are not to be caught.After lunch, Aniruddha sat down with his diary, he was trying to figure out the true meaning of the verse.For a long time, he wrote and looked away once in a while to see if the monk was coming. Suddenly a sound came from the border of the forest, a new guest, it seems that there will be a trial again. He went out of the room to see what happened. He saw the postman had come, followed by two forest guards, as he was taking him to the headman, aniruddha showed his hand and said, "Stop, don't disturb the headman always." Go, go for duty again. Leave him. He is a postman, all you will bring them forward when he returns from here. Aniruddha asked the postman, is your bicycle out of the forest? Postman said, yes, but you have mail from your home. Your mother has a fever again, and your sister is asking for your help. To be taken to the hospital. If you come with me, that's fine On hearing this, he immediately went back inside and took a 15-day leave at the head office by satellite phone.He also said that he would send a man here temporarily for daily satellite attendance duty. Then he went to the headman and told him that he would send someone instead for 15 days and that he should be allowed to enter.headman removed a bone locket from his neck and handed it to aniruddha`s hand and said, "If we see it, we will let someone in." The seven immortals bless your all, Go. Then he and the postman proceeded outside the forest. The environment outside the forest is a bit different. The hot heat of the sun is touching Aniruddha's body. He brought his watch with him; he will go there and fix it at the neighbourhood shop. Both of them have a long way to go now. Only one bus passes through this road every day. The postman has a bicycle, yet he walks with Aniruddha Aniruddha suddenly stopped and said

-you can go ahead. Maybe someone is waiting for you now. The postman smiled, said thanks, rang the bell twice,

And pushed the bicycle forward. But now He has to walk a long way alone. if any vehicle passes through this road, he can go quickly. Now he has come far from the forest. The temperature has dropped a bit, and it will be afternoon. Now he has walked only 5 km. Still, about 45 km to go. Now he has to stand for a while because it is not possible to walk so far without a car. A cargo truck was approaching from a distance, he felt a little relieved. Aniruddha raised his hand and stopped the truck. Requested the driver if he could be moved a little further

The driver said, come. Not many cars pass through this road because, This road is unpaved and has a few bumps. It does not fix because, moreover, there is another straight path to the destination, it was made by theForeigners, and god knows, in what sense they did this road, but it was more advantageous for Aniruddha. deep forest on both sides of the road. Now he came to a private bus stand. Now he arrives bus stand. Thanked the driver. The driver welcomed and went ahead. Some vans were parked there. He decided to go with one of them. He called the van driver and got into the van after bargaining. Now he will go straight home after some distance there is another bus stand from there he will take some fruit and sweets. He keeps some money, such as car rentals and other purchases.

Now he stopped the van and purchased some vegetables and some duck meat, then he got back in the van. After some time she came in front of the house. Her younger sister Kamala was standing at the door, she was very happy to see Elder Brother. She said -brother, what have you brought for me? He said, a lot of things and took the two bags from the van, and entered the home. He came home and saw that Saraswati had also come. He handed a bag to Saraswati and said, there are some vegetables, meat, fruits, and sweets inside, keep them in the kitchen, and give me some water. Kamala gave water, and Daima was lying there, Aniruddha put her hands on her head and asked, how are you now? Daima says you have come, now I am feeling better. The van is standing outside because He has already told the driver that he will take his mother to the hospital with this van. Now he said to Daima, -let's go, the van is standing outside, you have to go to the hospital.

Kamala and Saraswati gently picked up their mother and took her into the van. Two sisters sat in the back seat, Daima lay in the middle and Aniruddha sited beside the driver. After some time they arrived at the hospital. The doctor saw his mother and said, Ok, she has a little fever, it will be fine once I have given some medicine. If the fever does not go away then a blood test should be done. Then the medicine was brought, and the doctor had already given an injection. Then he took Daima home again, and after paying all his fare to the van driver, he sat for a while, it was ten o'clock at night. Saraswati cooking, Kamala helping infrequently to elder sister. Aniruddha brought many things to Kamala and Saraswati, they were very happy to get the various ornaments, garlands, and stones made by the tribals. Apart from that he told his sisters that he will take them to the market tomorrow.

Today is Monday, It's morning now. He slept very well last night. Now he has to go to Shyam's house. There was no time yesterday. If Shyam knew that aniruddha came so he would surely meet him. Now it's 10`o clock morning, and Aniruddha goes to Shyam. Shyam is a young man from his neighboring village. Last year he passed the college final. He is also trying for a forest department job. He greatly respects Aniruddha, He had done his "National Cadet Corps" training so he can do a lot of hard work like aiming and gun firing, survival in the forest, etc. He saw Aniruddha and came running. He was feeding the cows. Come and said, sir, when you came, you could have told me, I go to you. Aniruddha said, no I came, you have to play a role this time. Shyam said, tell me what the role is, I agree. Aniruddha said you have to stay for 15 days in the forest where I work. I will give you fifteen days' salary.

Shyam said I agree.

Aniruddha said You leave tomorrow morning. Go and make a satellite phone for attendance, and yes, take this tribal locket, it is your identification. they won't let you enter the forest without it. Be very careful, don't talk too much to them, only listen to what they saying. Oh, don't worry. This is your first experience, they can have some fun with you. You assure them you are an honest man. Okay bye. Tomorrow we will meet at the bus stand. Aniruddha came home, now it's noon. his mother was now healthy, sitting up. He was happy to see them and said, there is no need to worry. You recovered and there is no need to worry. Daima said I have a thought, If we get a good boy for Kamala then I will get peace. Kamla studies college, but she is not willing to marry now. Aniruddha said, you don't have to worry about that, I know a good boy. I will show you At the perfect time. Now let Kamala complete her studies. When my salary was low then, I could not make Saraswati well-educated. But this should not be the same with Kamala.

He asked Kamala, who was standing next to him, "Am I right?"

Kamala said, yes. but I want to get a job. I mean I want nursing training, but this is much more costly if I get a scholarship so I can continue my study to get the job. aniruddha said, okay it is not a problem, if you do not get a scholarship then don't think too much I will apply for the nursing scheme. Don't be in tension.

Kamala was happy. Saraswati has tears in her eyes. Aniruddha asked Saraswati, why are you crying, you made me guilty. I couldn't make you study in college. I am sorry. But you still have time, you can complete your graduation. Want to study again? Saraswati Said, No brother, No more by me, but one thing would be if I could take a sewing course, this is not much costly but My husband drives a car and takes care of the family, you know many people at our home. so without any scholarship, it is not possible. Aniruddha said, don't worry, you know Central has launched a free sewing course.

15 days passed, and in these few days aniruddha did many important responsibilities, Saraswati has been admitted to the sewing course, and Daima is now healthy. Now he has to go, these few days they enjoyed much, but from this time everything will be like before. Saraswati will go to her husband's house, now only Kamala and Daima will remain in the house.

Aniruddha has entered the forest. Shyam will go back to his house in that car. So the car is still standing.

As Aniruddha comes back here, the tribals start playing drums again, they welcome him with flower garlands, he doesn't recognize Shyam, he is dressed like them. Now he said to Shyam, let's you return, the car is parked outside the forest. Shyam says I want to stay here with you sir.

Aniruddha says no it's not possible you have to go home. your mom is tensed. I will call again when the time calls for your help. You return the headman's locket.

Shyam returned his locket to the headman. And said goodbye to everyone

headman asked Aniruddha, what is your objection? when we have no objection if he wants to stay?

-Headman, I am sorry to say, his mother has given an order that he can not disobey. Like here, nobody can disobey your orders. As these conversations were underway, a loud explosion suddenly shattered the peace. The blast came from the western side of the forest. Aniruddha now faces a dilemma as his responsibilities have increased and he must choose between a job and a personal pursuit. He is unable to make a decision and is struggling with the weight of his choices.

Meanwhile, the monk has reappeared and is cautioning everyone that the present moment is not suitable for Shyam's departure. Shyam is needed and it falls upon the monk to persuade Shyam's parents. He vows to put forth his best effort in communicating this to them. The monk spoke to Aniruddha and informed him that he must be introduced to a source of power. He then addressed the chief and instructed him to remain in a state of readiness and to accompany everyone to that location. The monk warned that there was great danger present in their current surroundings. Evacuate the women and children to a safe place immediately. "Shyam, bring your firearms with you. We must set out towards the east immediately. I instruct all of the tribal soldiers to equip themselves with poisoned arrows instead of regular ones and to safeguard their communities. Four of you, accompany us. come on".

Once Aniruddha went to his house. On a piece of paper, he wrote, "To the driver, Get out from here as soon as possible. There is a problem here." Hey if you don't have any problem. If you want to do something for the country, just take the car and come into the forest, we will wait for 5 minutes.

Then wrapped the paper in a blue stone and handed it to a guard and said to throw it to the driver standing outside the forest. And if he wants to come, let him come. We need everyone now. After some time, the driver came into the forest with his car. The driver said I have extra oil in my car, no need to worry about that. I am ready to sacrifice for the country. Aniruddha said Shyam and Sanyasi to sit in this car, He then ran into the house, carrying a box of ammunition and a satellite phone into the car. Then he got into the car, luckily the car was big, there is a lot of space there so four more people could sit easily. The four were not used to sitting in the car and felt hesitant but Aniruddha closed the door and told them to proceed. The car moved eastward, cutting through the small weeds along the small dirt road. A fire could be seen going some distance, which means a bomb had exploded. A guard was lying on the ground. Anirudh asked the car to stop. He got out of the car and went towards the man. The man was breathing. The guard is trying to say something but he has no strength to get up, his legs are paralyzed, aniruddha asks what did you see, tell me. He said that he had seen a strange man a while ago, as he described it as if some otherworldly presence had arrived, and as he tried to speak, he fainted. Aniruddha raised his hand towards the car and asked 2 guards to pick him up and get into the car He was somehow lifted into a carriage. Then, Aniruddha described the man to the monk,

The monk said the guard,- The underworld king has come. The guard regains consciousness he tells the other guards. When I was going, I saw a person passing through the forest, I thought it was a thief, I didn't understand that much, I went ahead and asked what are you doing in the forest at such a late night? Then he said I need to go this way don't stop me. I said -you will not be allowed to enter the forest.

Saying this, his eyes lit up. I have been in this condition ever since

The monk said that anyway, the man needs to be found, he has come to find a object which is in an old temple in this forest.

Now Aniruddar remembered that glass, he said to the monk, well, have you managed to recover some of the verses written on that glass?

The monk said yes, and, it is related to this event. The great majesty of the underworld wanted to confuse us by revealing the truth. He thought that as long as we investigate these things, they will take the object from the old temple to the underworld. But that won't happen. I guessed something like this earlier

The monk started to show the driver the way to the old temple. The car moved along the road for a long time, and the front of the car had a lot of scratches. The car stopped in front of the old temple. There are so many bushes and forests around because it is not a locality, it is an old temple far away where no one comes to worship anymore. The earlier public used to come to offer puja once a day but now there is a new temple in the village so everyone goes there because there are big poisonous snakes here. Everyone got out of the car.

A guard said, a long time ago, During the time of Chandraditya, there was a dense population outside this forest. This temple became cursed after a man cut his hand and gave blood there. And everyone is forced to leave that village and go elsewhere. This is recorded in our old manuscript. headman knows better about this matter. Because three of his generation have recorded this story. Kings used to come here to worship. Some places are lying like ruins over time everything is getting faded and one day maybe the temple will collapse.

A bell hangs on the door, the door is made in Vedic form, half broken and half stuck inside the bell hangs.

Aniruddha rang the bell once, and immediately more than a thousand spoonbills came out with noise. A stench arose, this smell resides where the spoonbill lives. Shyam and the driver have rulers in each hand. They continued to move towards the temple by breaking the branches on both sides with those rulers.Four guards stood outside. The monk asked the driver to stay outside and said he would get in himself. Shyam sometimes looked for snakes. Not only are there terrible snakes here, but there are also many poisonous crabs that rule here. The temple is surrounded by forest. Aniruddha said to the driver. Keep the windows of the car closed so that no snake or bug gets into the car. Aniruddha took out the gun from his waist. aniruddha doesn't keep a gun with him of course he is given a gun but his gun stays in his office. But today he brought it. This is not much use because there is no project. A gun should only be kept for self-safety if there is some miscreant or thief bandit in the forest, it is not for killing, but for self-defense. But aniruddha thinks that he can protect himself and he doesn't need a gun so he doesn't keep it. Se gun pointed at the door of the temple and walked slowly. On his right side is the monk and on the left side is shyam.

Aniruddha asked "if there was anyone" As soon as he asked, several pairs of pigeons went out. There is silence all around, only the chirping of bats, the sound of birds, the sound of various small insects, and spiders, and nothing else. Now everyone entered the temple. There are two new lamps on the side. They are impure. There is a huge idol of lord Bhairava in front. lord Bhairav Nath's vehicle dog is also there.various crafts on the wall. The craft of churning the sea, followed by images of various gods and goddesses. There are also many nude body art dancers. Roughly the whole temple is decorated with terracotta. Aniruddha already knew about this terracotta. So aniruddha began to look at the terracotta's very closely as if searching for something in them.

Shyam asked. Sir, what is here?

aniruddha said I recovered the spell written on the glass.

The monk said what do you mean that this temple is connected with this spell??

Aniruddha said, yes, you are right. but You couldn't understand, I knew it at home. But I didn't say anything about this. I was verifying it, I thought it was a sign when you sat in the car and suspected it was a move. Look at this - पञ्चमणि बल्ल्युक्त धारणे महामहिमा । means having precious stone like Panchamani, having that power and महामहिमा mean chieftain, the great leader. what is the whole line, father?

"The head who possesses the power of Panchamani". देवप्रिया श्रीयुक्ता असुरलोके प्रोपुजिता। । Here is देवप्रिया – it means beloved of lord of all gods and श्रीयुक्ता means highly respected and असुरलोके प्रोपुजिता i.e. one who is worshiped by the demons. That is, what is the whole line? Beloved and revered by the lord of all gods and worshiped by the Asuras.

सः दूरतः पश्यति, it means, He sees from afar. अंगकिार देवस्य समीपम् असमक अखलि-बन्धव..

अंगकिार देवस्य समीपम्- That is, asking the lord of god to give a promise, असमक अखलि-बन्धव means our friends god of the world.

Father, you were saying that you do not understand this god. "The head who possesses the power of Panchamani" It is said in the 108 names of this god who calls Friend god by that name. Take a look at, who gave this name to this god. . Shukracharya named Akhil Bandhav. So what does the whole mean? Guru sukrachrya holds the power of Panchamani. The most beloved and respected lord of god and who is worshiped by the demon but he is a son of Bhrigu Rishi and Kavyamata. has seen some secret messages from afar where our friend god is asking the lord of god to speak about some secret matter. Now the question is, what was the promise, Friend god asking from the lord of god? Here is such an image of the friend god praying to the lord of the gods. Hay's father look at this design that is exactly matching with the verse, lord of god is sitting in blessing posture, and Friend god is kneeling and bowing and saying something. See shyam under every terracotta but many words are written but only under this terracotta nothing is written. Do you understand where the secret is?

The monk said, my efforts for so many years were in vain, I could not understand such a simple thing. Aniruddha says no father it is not that, I live here but I don't know about this temple. Even though you are an outsider, you know it. But how did you know it?

The monk said I came here long years ago. Maybe you weren't born then. When the ancient headman was oppressing their people, I had to come. I took him with me. Then again peace was established here. Now his descendants live in some parts of the Himalayas. So the headman told me about the history of this temple. Peace was established here, but there was no one to lead, so there was a fierce war during the foreign period. Many tribes were killed by their ammunition. A hand-counted tribal were spending their life here with fear. Then a boy got the blessing of seven immortals and became powerful. He was the father of this present Headman Mallana. His father's name was Rihushula, this is a historic name mentioned in tribe history for his good leadership, he drove the foreign out of this forest. Since then this forest is kept secret, and some books are written, the forest natives do not allow anyone to come here for this cursed temple. But this is completely false. The truth is that there are many expensive organic medicines in this forest. And there is a substance that Rihushula holds in his neck. The real power in it is believed to be hidden somewhere in this temple before his death. Only a piece of it is worn around the neck of the current headman Mallana. Shyam asks, then what if I had a piece of it? The monk said, "Yes,

shyam said so it has a rough edge on one side. I thought it was broken. Aniruddha says we have to find this as soon as possible and should be given to the headman.

Sir, what is it? asked Shyam.

Aniruddha and father didn't notice until now that there was a yantra under that terracotta. He inspected it very carefully with a feather than a crease appeared on his forehead suddenly said Sukra Yantra! What is it doing here? Aniruddha stuck his hand in the middle of the Yantra and it opened like a drawer. As soon as the drawer opened, the entire temple shook with a loud noise A guard came from outside and said we have to leave soon, someone is coming from far away. His skin color is black like coal. The monk said The king of the underworld is coming, we cannot fight with him in this state, let them go from here. Shyam didn't say anything even when he said something. Aniruddha said to the driver, let's not stay here anymore, now we have to go from there. let's go...quick. Shyam quickly took the picture of that terracotta and then quickly ran out of there, a big stone came from nowhere and fell in front of them, and only a little. It was worn by someone. Coming in front of the car, the windows of the car were broken with stones, now the stones started coming from all around, and eight people including the driver started saving themselves, Shyam once took out the gun and fired a shot into the sky The sound of gunshots caused all the birds to fly away from there. Did the stones stop coming.

Anirudda said...What did you do? Don't be stupid, keep the gun. Let's get into the car quickly, driver, start the car, quick, quick, quick. The driver quickly got into the car and started it but the car didn't start, the driver started pounding the steering wheel. Everyone got into the car, but the rocks didn't stop coming. The big rocks came crashing into the car. The window panes were broken, so everyone sat down. A rock hit the driver's forehead and immediately the driver's head burst and blood started coming out.aniruddha immediately tied his shirt to his head, then laid the driver down and took the steering wheel himself, after pulling the key three times, the car started, quickly turned the steering wheel and started to back the car, another rock came close to anirudda's forehead. And the forehead would have split if it was a little bit, while Shyam's hand was bleeding in a storm. Aniruddha unconsciously drives the car through the bushes at high speed, after some time the car starts to reduce the speed slowly, by now the car is far away from the old temple. The rocks have also stopped coming.

shyam asked to the monk, what happened to us, father?

The monk said, I will say later that we have to go to the hospital now. Go along this road, there is a hospital near, but I don't know if there is a doctor.. but I am sure there will be some medicine or bandage. The rate at which blood is coming out of the driver's head, if he is not taken to the hospital very soon, maybe a disaster. After some time, the car entered the hospital. aniruddha quickly got down from the car and started breaking the door of the hospital, which was closed. Shyam laid the driver in a bed and the monk immediately came and started treating the driver. First, he untied the shirt from the driver's head, bleeding so much that it was not visible to the eyes, and started to clean the blood from the driver's head.

The monk said, Must be stitched. A lot has passed.

Aniruddha bandaged Shyam's hand. He got a lot of injuries on his hand. The driver got stitches on his head. He is sleeping. aniruddha is sitting on a chair. He feels guilty. Shyam is sitting with his head down. Until then a storm blew. What happened from where?.

aniruddha held Shyam's hand and said, sorry, brother, it happened for me. Why did I involve you with this!! I feel bad brother. I am thinking about how to show my face to the driver's parents.

Shyam said, don't worry about me sir, I come with my responsibility, your duty means our duty, there is nothing to feel bad about it sir, The driver has regained consciousness, and he can walk, he says he can walk, but he will not be released now, he will be kept in the forest office for 2 days and then sent with Shyam.

Now the monk said, let's go to the forest.

Aniruddha drove the car. Because the driver was injured. The car went straight into the forest. Everyone came and saw that there was a war there. The monk said that the king of the underworld has come here in search of us. In time tribals went to a safe place so he could not harm anyone, only some houses were damaged, and it is not known whether he is still in the forest or not. Even during that time in the old temple Aniruddha had filled that object in his pocket, now he gave it to the monk and said. -See if this is it.

The monk said yes that is it but hide it now, If he was here somewhere, it would not be difficult for him to snatch it. He also entered Anirudd's house All things are scattered. A foul stench is coming, just like there is a mole nearby.

Today is the second day, and the driver is now healthy than before, and he said he can drive the car, It's very important to return home today. At the same time, Shyam will be going with the driver. He was not willing but Aniruddha and Sannyasi both forced him. Last night Headman treated Driver and gave him medicine with various herbs for internal and external use, He wrapped some medicine in big leaves for future use, Such as antibiotics, antiseptics, sleeping, cough, head pen, etc. The driver also cleverly collected some fresh buds from the headman, which he will consume later. Headman says it is a great medicine. He mentioned that he learned about from Aniruddha, who had read about it in a magazine. "This substance is legal in many countries and is even sold by shop owners like medicine." During their visit, the headman also offered Shyam and the driver, some of his favorite organic perfume and fresh honey. Now, with their visit over, the driver needs to fix the car before they can continue on their journey." He didn't take a single penny from aniruddha. But Anirudha forcefully gives him three thousend rupees, which is nothing for him. Three hours passed, and they returned home. Anirudh has arranged a very important meeting in the forest court. There were the Headman, Aniruddha, four special advisers, two vice-headman, three medicine makers, seven head of forest guard and a court poet besides, and the whole clan. Various safeguards are being discussed in this meeting today.

Headman asked, what is the main reason for today's meeting?

Aniruddha stood up from his seat and bowed to the headman and asked permission. headman saw his hand and gave permission. Aniruddha took the object from his pocket and showed it to everyone and said.

-I Hope you all are looking this object well, can anyone tell me, what is this? Headman ? are you know?

Surprised headman got up from the throne, tears in his eyes. As he had seen something he never thought he would see again.

Aniruddha said This is the Object, which our headman`s headman Rihushul received as a blessing from seven immortals and he used to hold it himself that we recover it from the old temple. It is believed that this object can possess supernatural powers. Everyone is looking at that object.

The poet said, Whatever you say, it's a lie. Because it disappeared after he died.

Aniruddha said, no it is not true, it did not disappear, rather there was no one to protect it. At that time of headman Rihusahul hide it in that temple. So that it does not fall into the hands of a bandit, government, scientist, or any other common man. Since it was given by God himself, it has no right to be preserved in any government museum. It is the property of the present Headman. And traditionally it will be considered the property of the next headman. Poet, you want proof, so? See.

Saying this, Aniruddha said to the headman, O headman, can you please give me your locket once?

Headman removed the locket from his neck and gave it to Aniruddha. Now Aniruddha said,

come here an ornament maker, please.

A jeweler came, Anirudha handed him the locket and said -please take it and separate this white part from the frame.

He separated it with his technical instruments. Now Aniruddha joined the locket with this object together and a light illuminated the entire courtyard, and in a moment the light was gone. Seeing this everyone was shocked including Headman. Everyone was so happy. As they started beating the drum, Aniruddha immediately raised his hand to stop the drum, and the drum stopped.

Aniruudha said, Please Stop the drums, now is not the moment of joy, For still, our enemy is near, And he's looking for this object, so he doesn't even realize we have this object. You are not familiar with his power, he is a demon. First, we need to keep it in a safe place. Then we have to face the demon, we all know there is a lot of bloodsheds possible. Because he is very powerful like a deity. So we cannot defeat him in ordinary war. In this case, we need the help of this object. If We return it to the seven Immortals, then we can be out of danger, or else we need to know first how this substance work against a demon.

The headman agreed and everyone understood it.

Headman said, We have an ancient book written in our language, which was written by my father Rihusahu himself.

Aniruddha said let that book be brought here. Bring the book. Now Aniruddha said to the poet,

-Now look in this book, whether there is any mention about how it will work.

The poet said I have read this book. It doesn't say how to activate it, but it says, "A devotee prays to our Lord, that, in this Koli era, no supernatural power may develop in the world, promise me please, The Lord is assuring the devotee that it will be so, no matter how much Meditation or ritual does in this Kali Era, but no one will possess any supernatural powers.

This time The monk looked at Aniruddha. Aniruddha understood There is a similarity between the words written in that glass, There is another puzzle in his mind that Guru Shukracharya appeared to Rihusahula. The monk understood his thoughts and shook his head and said,

- you are right. He also told me that he was once face to face with Shukracharya when he got this object from seven immortals.

Now the poet said yes, Ruhusahula wrote in this book, I met the master of the demon in this ancient Lord's temple, he told me, Lord said that this object can be used only for once, then it will turn into a natural stone, which can never be used again in the Koli era.

A calm atmosphere has been created in the court. Everyone is quite worried.

Now the Headman said, everyone listens carefully, It is the order of the court. None of us will take responsibility for this object; we will surrender it to seven immortal gods so that this destructive force does not disturb our public life. Although it can only be used once. And if it is activated in any way, I think this forest will be burnt down. Therefore, this forest court is coming to the decision, this object will not be handed over to the government, nor we will hold it in our neck traditionally, nor we will use force in any circumstances. Keeping in mind the promise made by the Lord to His devotee, we will not use any supernatural power in this Koli era. So this object will be handed over to god seven immortal as soon as possible. OK? Even then, if we have to fight with a demon, we will fight with our natural strength.Now we will all go to the place where seven immortal is meditating, No one else will go there except the three of us. Now everyone can exit from the court.

Aniruddha will meet the seven immortals again. But the monk said aniruddha, He would not do as before, and he also said that this object will surrender by the headman only. We will be neutral spectators.

Now it is evening, and the three of them are walking in the forest, They are also slightly afraid if that demon comes and goes away with it. And he goes and snatches it from them. The sounds of different animals in the forest, different sounds are fueling that fear. The stench has slowly started again, which means he is present in this Forrest. They are walking a long way. Headman put some fragnance on all of us. He won't smell us.The monk said

-that's not possible, if he wants to kill us, then no smell is protecting us

The three are walking fearfully in the deep forest. no one knows what will happen. The monk is chanting a mantra. After some time the monk said we have come near now. Without saying a word, a foul smell made everyone close their noses. The light in the headman's hand began to flicker. The monk said, he has come, at this moment we have to keep a cool head and work so that there is no war. Suddenly a flute sounds trying to knock them unconscious, a very sweet flute sound. The monk said to cover your ears

As the three were now standing, a hulking devil with a blue light suddenly appeared in front of them.

The devil said, give me that object, I will leave or I can destroy the whole forest now.

The monk said you are so powerful an underworld king. Who did you come from the underworld to get one little thing? No, I don't believe you, you have any other purpose. You will not be bored with it.

The devil said we can come to this earth only when some supernatural power exists on this planet as per natural law, you know very well that, So quickly give me this object without any discussion.

Aniruddha and Headman understood well that the monk is trying to cheat on the devil. But it remains to be seen whether they will succeed in this.With a roar, the devil said again,

-don't talk again. give the object quickly otherwise, I will kill all of you.

Now the monk wisely said, no, no, no, you making a mistake, do you think we are afraid of your threats?Listen, if we die, that object will become useless.

Now it seems that the monk can trap the devil bit by bit in his mental web. The devil is a little worried now.

Anirudda boldly said with fear, Such a disciple of such a wise teacher?

The monk said,-Woe to you for such behavior. Whom do you hate all the deities yet you come to take their things?

The devil said it is not a thing of the deity. The account of the churning of the sea is still left. During the churning of the ocean, deities cheated us and took away many things.

The monk said, But it did not come from the churning of the sea.

The devil roar again and said, you are talking too much. Now Give me the object or I will snatch it away from you.

The monk said,- Okey, no problem, but know this too. Even if you do that, it will be useless, your coming this far will be in vain. whose property it is, If he doesn't willingly give it to you, you can't do anything, so stop yelling and talking coolly, we're not afraid of you.

Now the king of demons is Trapped by the monk.

The devil asked- then tell me what should I do?

The monk said, now come to the point. Well, tell who gave you this idea means who encouraged you to this object? What is his opinion about this object?

The devil has now assumed the form of a human being, the monk has trapped him in such a way, That he can't understand what was going to happen to him.The three are walking forward.And the devil going backward with looking at their faces. He does not walk looking ahead. He keeps saying, Laladro encouraged me, he is a special guest of our demon world, he comes from the land of the black angel, according to him if we get this, we can rule your world.

By the time they reached their destination, the yantra is visible in front, but Aniruddha could not see the Seven Immortals now, the lamps were shining. The devil hasn't seen the front yet. devil just keeps saying

Now headman said, I will urinate. I come from that side. but The devil has no eye on that, Headman walks forward and prays to seven immortals while Aniruddha and the monk listen to the devil's speech.

the other side headman will placing the object on the Kali yantra and immediately the devil looks ahead. As soon as he looked ahead, the monk and Aniruddha hid behind, and shouted to the headman,

-"Put it in the kali yantra, quickly."

The devil has caught their trick now, he will march forward in anger, And then Headman placed that object on the kali yantra. Now a strange light from that Kali yantra made the whole forest shine like day time.The devil has disappeared. Oh, he has no power to come into this world again. This time all three looking at the seven immortals. But no one can approach them. Because it is an act against the rules. They are bowing from afar. The monk said,

"Look, my son, your soul is meditating somewhere like them." Aniruddha asked, can I see it?

The monk said,- yes you can see but you have to find it yourself.

They are going back again.

After 10 years,

That forest has the same. The monk was not seen after that day, he may be gone back to the Himalayas The headman is sitting on a rock and smoking cannabis, and small boys and girls are playing. Aniruddha's Daima died 4 years ago. Aniruddha appealed to the government to build Ayurvedic health care near this forest. Gov kept his promise to a build small health center, where his sister is now Dr. Kamala, provides first aid to everyone. He also kept some tribal nurses there. Aniruddha got married, He and his wife Anindita live here. Shyam has now got a job in this forest office. He is in love with Kamala, they will get married next year.

Endless

As with any creative work, the possibilities are endless, and I am excited to see where my imagination takes me next. Perhaps a new story will emerge from these pages, or maybe a completely new idea will take root in my mind. I will continue to explore the realms of science and spirituality, and see what new adventures await me.In the meantime, I encourage you to keep your own imagination alive, and to never stop exploring the possibilities that lie within. Whether it be through reading, writing, or any other form of creative expression, let your mind run free and see where it takes you.

Thank you again for taking the time to read my story, and I wish you all the best in your own creative endeavors.

9 798889 862055

Printed by Libri Plureos GmbH in Hamburg,
Germany